Splat the Cat

For Maggie and her very own Splat cats—Spatz and Strawberry.
—R.S.

Special thanks to Maria.

More fantastic books by Rob Scotton

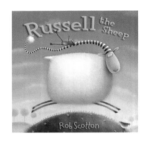   

www.robscotton.com

First published in hardback by HarperCollins Publishers, USA, in 2008
First published in paperback in Great Britain by HarperCollins Children's Books in 2008
This edition is produced exclusively for Bookstart

10 9 8 7 6 5 4 3 2 1

ISBN-13: 978-0-00-787827-7

HarperCollins Children's Books is a division of HarperCollins Publishers Ltd.

Text and illustrations copyright © Rob Scotton 2008

Typography by Neil Swabb

Visit our website at www.harpercollins.co.uk

Printed and bound by 1010 Printing International Ltd. ,China

HarperCollins Children's Books proudly supports Bookstart

Rob Scotton

Splat the Cat

HarperCollins *Children's Books*

*I*t was early in the morning
and Splat was wide awake.
Today was his first day at Cat School
and his tail wiggled wildly with worry.

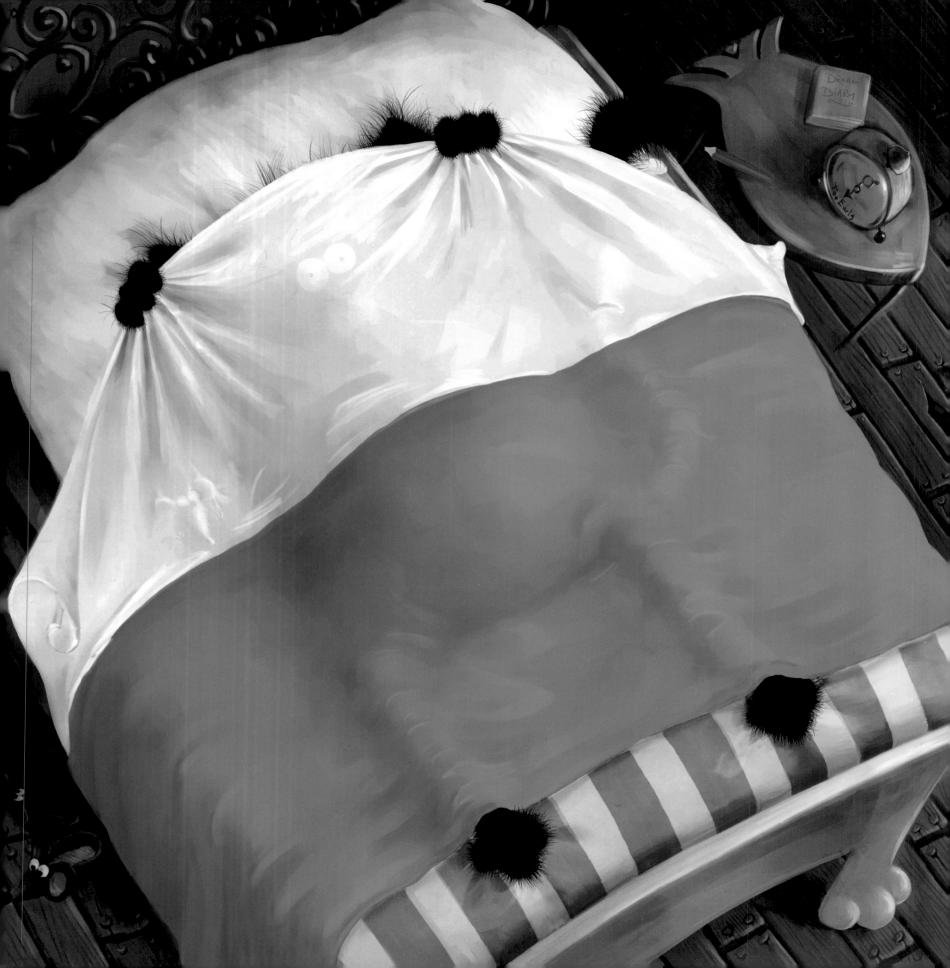

If I hide from the day, maybe it'll go away, he thought.

It didn't go away.

"Time to get up," said his mum.

"Time to get dressed," said his mum.

"I don't have any clean socks, Mum.
Maybe I should go to school tomorrow instead?" said Splat.

"You don't wear socks," said his mum.

"I'm having a bad hair day, Mum.
Maybe I should go to school
tomorrow instead?" said Splat.

His mum combed his hair.
"Purr-fect!" she said.

"Don't forget your lunch box," said his mum.

I'll need a friend today, thought Splat.

And he dropped his pet mouse, Seymour, into his lunch box.

"Time to go," said his mum.

"The front door won't let me out, Mum."

"The gate won't let go of my fingers, Mum."

"The lamppost won't get out of my way, Mum."

"MUM!"

"You can ride your bike if you like, Splat," said his mum.

So he did. But he didn't say a single word.

"Welcome to Cat School," said a big, round cat.
"I'm Mrs Wimpydimple, your teacher."

Splat's mum gave him a hug.
"I'll be back soon," she said.
"You'll be fine."

"Everyone, this is Splat.
Let's welcome him
into our class," said
Mrs Wimpydimple.

"Hi,

Mrs Wimpydimple began. "Cats are amazing," she said.

"We're clever, cunning and quick."

"Am I amazing too?" asked Splat.

"Yes, you too," said Mrs Wimpydimple.

"Cats climb trees, drink milk and chase mice," she continued.

"Why do we chase mice?" asked Splat.
"It's what we do," replied Mrs Wimpydimple.

"Why?" asked Splat.
"Because."

"Why?"

"Why?"

"Why?"

"Why?"

Mrs Wimpydimple sighed.
"Lunch time!" she announced.

Splat opened his lunch box.

"Mouse!"

The cats did what cats do.

Seymour hid behind a glass bottle,

and when the cats saw
his face through the glass,

they screamed and ran away.

Seymour did what
all mice want to do.

"Stop!" cried Splat.

"SPLAT!"

They didn't stop.

"Enough!" Mrs Wimpydimple said, and it ended. "It's milk time."

"Hurray!"

But the door to the milk cupboard was stuck.
"No milk today," announced Mrs Wimpydimple.

"AWWWW."

Splat whispered into Seymour's ear.
Seymour nodded and then...

A moment later,
the door swung open.

"Yum!"

Mrs Wimpydimple wrote again on the blackboard.

Cats don't chase mice

"Hurray!" cheered the class.

Soon it was home time.
Splat's mum returned and gave him a hug.

"I've got lots of friends...

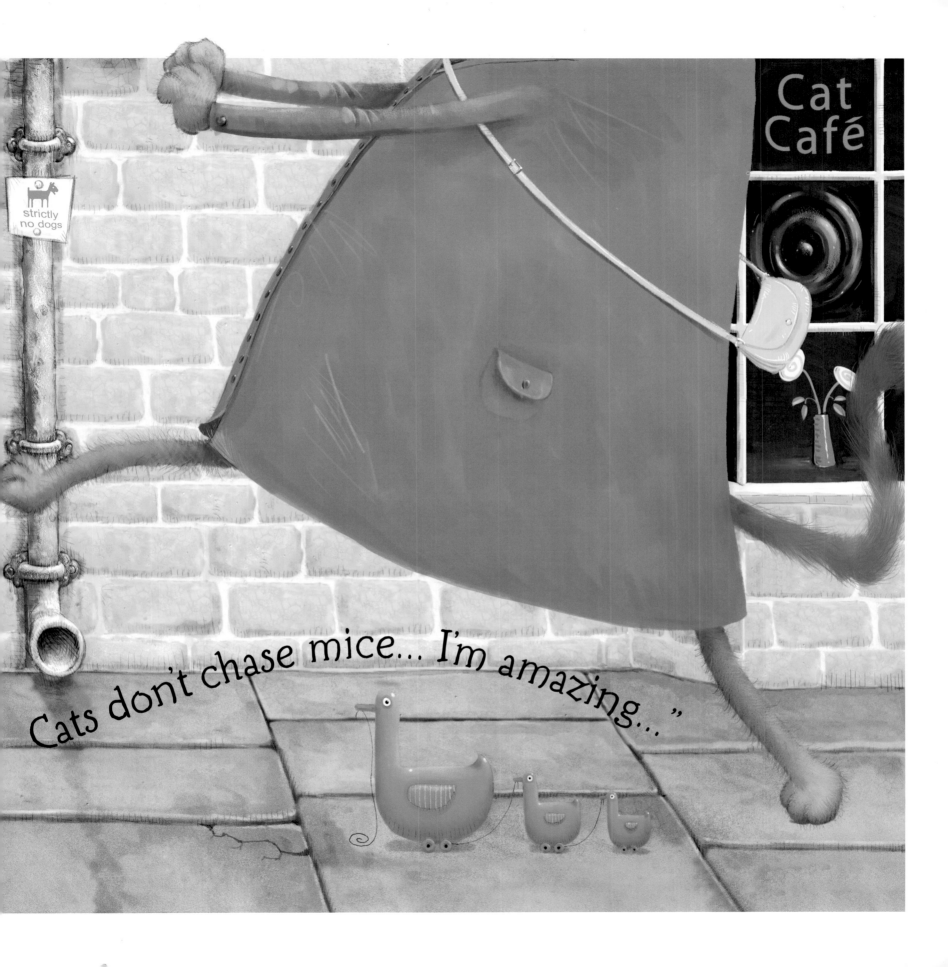

It was early the next morning
and Splat was wide awake.
Today was his second day at Cat School
and his tail wiggled wildly...
...with excitement.